ALEX VS FOUR-HEADED GARGANTUAN

LAURA PEETOOM

KEVIN FRANK

JAMES LORIMER & COMPANY LTD., PUBLISHERS
TORONTO

James Lorimer & Company Ltd., Publishers acknowledges the support of the
Ontario Arts Council. We acknowledge the support of the Canada Council for the
Arts which last year invested $24.3 million in writing and publishing throughout
Canada. We acknowledge the Government of Ontario through the Ontario Media
Development Corporation's Ontario Book Initiative.

Cover Design: Meredith Bangay

Library and Archives Canada Cataloguing in Publication

Peetoom, Laura, author
    Alex vs. the four-headed gargantuan / Laura Peetoom ; illustrated
by Kevin Frank.

Issued in print and electronic formats.
ISBN 978-1-4594-0957-6 (paperback).--ISBN 978-1-4594-0959-0 (epub)

    I. Frank, Kevin, 1962-, illustrator II. Title.

PS8631.E41A65 2015   jC813'.6   C2015-903813-8
                                    C2015-903814-6

James Lorimer & Company Ltd., Publishers 317 Adelaide Street West, Suite 1002 Toronto, ON, Canada M5V 1P9 www.lorimer.ca	Canadian edition (978-1-4594-0957-6) distributed by: Formac Lorimer Books 5502 Atlantic Street Halifax, NS, Canada B3H 1G4	American edition (978-1-4594-0958-3) distributed by: Lerner Publishing Group 1251 Washington Ave N Minneapolis, MN, USA 55401

Printed and bound in Canada.
Manufactured by Friesens Corporation in Altona, Manitoba, Canada
in August 2015
Job #215807

To Jenny and her crew, Super Paperboy's first fans — with a tip of the cap to the Peterborough Examiner *and our own super paperboy for the inspiration. Thanks!*

CONTENTS

THE MOUNTAINSIDE QUAKES AND RUMBLES.

THE WHIRLING COLUMN TAKES A NEW SHAPE, A STRANGE FORM.

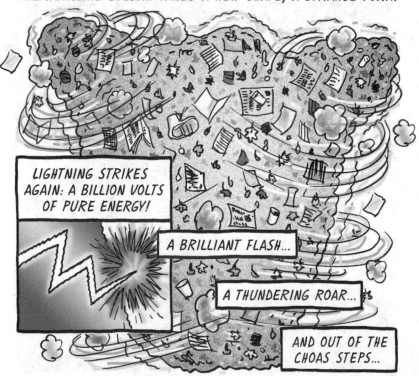

1
A HERO IS BORN

How would you like to earn some REAL money?
A newspaper route is available NOW
in YOUR neighbourhood.

Call Dave
(555) 731-3588

The school year had just started when the notice came. The newspaper wasn't the free one that everyone got twice a week. It was the *Clarion*, for which people paid and which was delivered every day except Sunday. Mom called the number and got the details: twenty-one papers, including their own, and all in the same block, practically. Their own block.

"What do you think, Alex? Do you want to give it a try?" Dad asked. He had had a paper route when he was a kid. Alex could see Dad wanted him to take it.

Alex was pretty sure he wanted to take it, too. Mom said he would make more than fifteen dollars a *week*. Alex was beginning to want a lot of things his parents had no clue about. And Alex's allowance was really small.

"He's just ten, though," Mom said, not so sure now that the paper route was becoming real. "It's a big responsibility."

"It'll be good for him. And I'll help," said Dad.

"He'll be going to strangers' *houses*," said Mom.

"We know half the people on our street, and he won't be going inside, ever," said Dad.

"I could take your cell phone, just in case," said Alex.

"In case of what?" asked Mom, alarmed.

"In case you're scared," said Alex.

Mom laughed. "Well, you can't do any worse than the last few carriers we've had," she said. "I don't know what's wrong with the service. It used to be much better."

Alex took the job. Dad went with him the first few times. The papers were heavy, but Alex liked the feeling of the bag on his shoulder. He felt taller carrying it, even though it bumped against his legs. He felt stronger, even though the weight of the papers made his shoulder ache.

The first time Alex went out by himself, the route seemed longer than it had with Dad. But Alex told himself to take it one house at a time. He nearly jumped out of his skin when the cell phone rang.

"Yes?"

"How's it going, honey?"

"Good."

"Do you remember the rules?"

Alex sighed. "Yes, Mom. Never go inside a house. Stick to the route. Call if I need help."

"That's right. Where are you now?

"Just turning on to Carl Avenue."

"Okay. I'll see you in a few minutes, then."

Alex had only two customers on Carl Avenue. He delivered to the first one, number 135, and then crossed the street to deliver to 132 — looking both ways, first, of course. As he came up the walk at number 132, a dog began to bark.

Alex didn't remember a dog from when Dad was with him. Was it new?

Alex opened the screen door. There was a hand-printed sign on the inside door.

Clarion Carrier:

Please fold newspaper and put in letter slot below.

Alex crouched down, lifted the letter slot cover, and peeked inside.

Yow! He fell backward in shock. *Wet red gums! Sharp white teeth!*

How was he going to get the paper in without getting his fingers bitten off?

Alex rolled the paper into a tube and flattened it. He lifted the slot cover again, and poked one end of the tube through. The barking became low, savage growling. Alex poked the tube in bit by bit. Just as the last centimetre was going in, the dog leaped, snapping.

Alex snatched his hand back and looked at it. His fingers were still there. He'd done it!

When Alex got home, his mom was waiting.

"Did it go all right?" she asked, helping him out with his paper bag.

"Fine," said Alex.

But Alex felt more than fine. He felt terrific. He felt like a superhero. Like . . . Super Paperboy!

THE SAVAGE YAPPER SNAPPER FROM THE CAVES OF CLAFOOEY WAS DREAMING. ITS LEGS TWITCHED AND ITS JAWS QUIVERED.

IN ITS DREAM, THE YAPPER SNAPPER LEAPS, THEN CLAMPS ITS JAWS ON THE NECK OF ITS HELPLESS PREY. DROOL MAKES A PUDDLE UNDER THE SLEEPING CREATURE'S JOWLS. THE DREAM YAPPER SNAPPER IS TEARING YUMMY MORSELS OF WARM MEAT FROM THE LIFELESS BODY OF ITS PREY.

SUDDENLY, THE SLEEPING YAPPER SNAPPER'S EARS PRICKED.

THERE IT WAS—THE SHUFFLE OF FOOTSTEPS OUTSIDE.

INSTANTLY AWAKE, THE SAVAGE YAPPER SNAPPER BOLTED TO ITS FEET. IT BEGAN TO TEMPT THE PREY TO COME INSIDE...

TO BE EATEN IS YOUR DESTINY!

YOU ARE FORTUNATE, O HUMAN. ONLY THE STRONGEST AND THE BEST ARE WORTHY TO BE THE FOOD OF THE MIGHTY YAPPER SNAPPER OF THE CAVES OF CLAFOOEY!

THE CAVE'S FEEDING SLOT INCHED OPEN...

AND THE YAPPER SNAPPER FELT THE FRENZY TAKE HOLD!

IT SNAPPED – AND THE LITTLE MORSELS THAT SMELLED SO DELICIOUSLY OF FRESH YOUNG HUMAN DISAPPEARED.

THE YAPPER SNAPPER'S JAWS CLOSED ON LIMP PAPER. ITS TONGUE TASTED ONLY DRY INK AND PAPER DUST.

HAH! SUPER PAPERBOY WINS AGAIN!

DISGUSTED, THE YAPPER SNAPPER SLUNK AWAY.

2
LOVELY, LOVELY CASH

A few weeks passed. Alex still had his fingers, and the empty QBrix container he used as a piggybank was getting nice and heavy.

One of the reasons Mom had let him take the job was that Alex didn't have to ring many doorbells. Most of his customers paid the newspaper office directly, so he didn't have to collect from them. The newspaper put the delivery payments right into the carriers' bank accounts.

Alex had been quite excited the day Dad took him to the bank to open his own account, during the week he started his route. He brought along five dollars from his birthday money for his first deposit. He and his dad signed the forms, and then the teller typed in all the information. While they waited, Alex enjoyed the thought of having a bank card, like his parents. He imagined walking up to an ATM, putting his card in the slot, and punching in his PIN. And then — oh! — all the lovely, lovely cash that would come out, all for him!

At last the teller was done. He handed Alex a newsletter, a page of stickers, and a little green book in a plastic sleeve. "Welcome aboard," he said. "Happy saving!"

"Where's my card?" Alex asked.

"What card?" said Dad.

"My ATM card. You know, so I can get cash out when I want to."

The teller looked at Dad, who shook his head and pulled Alex away from the counter.

"Alex, your mother and I talked about that. We feel that everything deposited by the newspaper office into your account should stay there.

That can be your savings, for really important things, such as a big school trip or something."

"What?" Alex cried.

"You can keep everything you collect door-to-door and do what you want with it," Dad told him.

"I'm only supposed to collect from three houses, though," said Alex. "And I deliver twenty-one papers. I'm not getting to keep very much." He saw all the lovely cash he'd imagined swirling down an enormous drain.

"You'll be keeping plenty," said Dad. "Most of what you earn, in fact, since you won't have to turn any of your collections to the newspaper. You see, the *Clarion* . . . blah-blah . . . statements . . . blah-blah . . . credit . . ."

Alex wasn't listening. He was thinking about all the things he liked about his newspaper route, things that had nothing to do with money.

He liked the walk, by himself, without any parents. He liked having a valuable job to do. He liked striding around the neighbourhood, feeling like he owned it. And, though he would never admit it to anyone, he liked being Super Paperboy.

Thursday was collection day. Alex collected from three customers. The first was an elderly couple — the Jurgenses, according to his route list. Mrs. Jurgens was usually home, and always had exactly the right amount ready, down to the last nickel: $4.50.

The second customer was never home. The third, Ms. Jain, was usually home, but didn't always have the right change.

Again, Dad went with Alex the first time he collected. Mom gave him some money to make change with, but when Alex gave Ms. Jain two quarters as change for her five, she handed them back.

"For the delivery boy," she told him.

Alex looked at Dad, and Dad nodded.

"Thank you," said Alex.

As they walked back to the sidewalk, Dad said, "Well, Alex, you just received your first tip. It won't be the last, either. Just wait until Christmas."

Thus Alex discovered Super Paperboy's Secret Source of Power.

The first time Alex collected by himself, Ms. Jain handed him a five-dollar bill again.

Oops. He had forgotten to bring change.

"I could come back later, when I've got some," he told Ms. Jain. "Or, you could pay me now and I'll just bring you back the change."

Ms. Jain laughed. "That's okay. My son used to deliver papers, and I know how much he loved getting tips. You just enjoy it, honey."

"Thanks!" said Alex.

The door had closed and Alex was on his way when he remembered Mrs. Jurgens. She had paid him with coins. He could have made change with them. He *should* have made change with them. He turned around.

"I forgot, I did have change," said Alex when Ms. Jain came to the door. "From another customer."

Ms. Jain looked at him hard. "You're honest. That's a good thing. Keep the five, honey."

Alex felt more than honest. He felt . . . super.

3
SUPER PAPERBOY GETS ROBBED

One Saturday, Alex studied the printout sitting on top of his newspaper stack. It had rows and columns of numbers with decimal points in them. He took it along on his route, trying to puzzle it out. The more he looked, the more minus signs he saw. When he got back, he brought the terrible piece of paper into the dining room.

"Dad," Alex said hollowly.

Dad looked up from the *Clarion* he was reading, and Alex handed him the printout. "It looks

SUPER PAPERBOY STOOD ON GOLD MOUNTAIN, HIS CAPE FLUTTERING LIKE A FLAG IN THE BREEZE.

SPREAD BELOW HIM WERE HIS DOMAINS: A TINY VILLAGE, PEACEFUL UNDER HIS WATCHFUL EYE; THE CAVES OF CLAFOOEY, QUIET FOR THE MOMENT; AND THE INNER WILDERNESS, WHICH HARBOURED DANGERS AND DELIGHTS HE HAD YET TO DISCOVER.

BEHIND AND ABOVE HIM, AT THE CREST OF GOLD MOUNTAIN, WAS THE CASTLE OF WONDERS. IT WAS A MIGHTY FORTRESS BUT IT, TOO, WOULD YIELD TO HIS POWERS IN TIME.

SUDDENLY, SUPER PAPERBOY FELT A STRANGE INNER TUG, A SUBTLE DRAINING OF HIS ENERGY. THE KILOMETRE TO HIS SECRET LAIR TOOK HIM SIX STRIDES TO COVER, INSTEAD OF HIS USUAL THREE.

AT THE THRESHOLD — HORRORS! — SUPER PAPERBOY STUMBLED!

WHAT EVIL MAGIC WAS THIS, SAPPING THE VERY SOURCE OF HIS SUPERPOWERS?

like I owe them money," he said. "Look at all those minus signs!"

Dad glanced at the printout and nodded. "That's your biweekly statement, the one I was telling you about. Remember, on the way home from the bank, when we set up your account?" When he saw Alex's blank look, he put down the newspaper and sighed.

"I'll explain it again," he said. "And listen this time."

"Make it simple," Alex pleaded. "I'm not an accountant like you."

Dad thought for a minute.

"Okay, I'll tell you how it worked when I was a paperboy. I collected from all my customers, every week. Every week, they paid me cash for the actual newspaper and for my delivering it. The money that paid for the actual paper went back to the newspaper office. I kept what was left over. Do you understand?"

Alex nodded.

"It's kind of the same for you, but it happens electronically. The customers who pay the

Clarion office directly are paying for their actual paper *and* for you delivering it. The *Clarion* keeps the cost of the paper and gives the delivery portion of the payment to you. That's the minus signs, here, because they are taking money out of their account and putting it in yours. The minus signs belong to the *Clarion*, not to you. Get it?"

Alex nodded again. So he didn't owe the *Clarion* money. Thank goodness!

"Good. Though I must say, this accounting method seems unnecessarily complicated. I wonder what program they're using? If *I* were doing it, I'd —"

"Dad. Focus," said Alex.

"Yes. Sorry. Where was I? Oh, yes. Look, just ignore this paper." He checked his phone. "We're too late today, but next week I'll take you to the bank to update your bankbook. Then you'll see."

Alex hurried through his route the following Saturday, and when he got back Dad took him to the bank to update his book. There were five columns: one with codes, one with dates, and three that Dad explained. One, called Credits, showed money coming in. The next column, called Debits, was for money going out. The third showed the balance — what was left when all the coming and going was done for the day.

"Money going out? How? You told me it had to stay in!" said Alex.

"Calm down. That column's empty, see? And it should stay that way."

Alex studied the bankbook. "There's only three *Clarion* deposits. I've been delivering for weeks!"

"Hey, go easy on us accountants!" said Dad. "Paycheques usually lag behind the calendar a little. The *Clarion* has to calculate what they owe you for delivering, subtract the cost of your collection customers' papers, and then add your flier earnings. I think they're doing pretty well paying you every week!" He started up the car. "And think of all the cash you've collected."

"Yeah, that's been okay," Alex admitted.

"Better than okay, I'd say," said Dad. "You

have plenty in that container in your bedroom. So, leave the bank balance to grow in peace. All right?"

The fifth Thursday, when Customer Never-Home was not home for the fifth time, Alex was struck by a thought. Customer Never-Home didn't pay the *Clarion* directly and he wasn't giving Alex any money, either. That meant that Alex was delivering for free! *And* paying for the actual papers!

"I'm being robbed!" Alex said at dinner.

"What?" cried his parents at the same time.

Alex said, "141 Abel Avenue hasn't paid me once. So who's paying for his papers? Me, that's who!"

Dad got up from the table and went into the office. He came back with Alex's *Clarion* carrier handbook.

"In the event of customer non-payment, the *Clarion* blah, blah, blah . . . Yes, here it is."

Dad studied the page for a while, then summed it up for Alex.

"You should have told the *Clarion* two weeks

THE MIGHTY TOME OF MAGIC WAS ACHIEVING ITS PURPOSE.
AS HE STUDIED THE RUNES WRITTEN THERE, SUPER PAPERBOY
FELT HIS POWER RETURNING. HE WAS BACK!

ago that 141 Abel Avenue wasn't paying. They'll cover three weeks' worth of papers for you, but that's it. So, if you don't get the money you're owed from number 141, you are indeed paying for his papers this week. And next week, too, if you don't stop delivering."

"I'll get the money," said Alex.

After dinner, Alex wrote a notice on the computer.

Dear Clarion-Stealing Criminal,

So, you must think you have a pretty good racket going, stealing papers from hardworking independent businessmen who are younger and smaller than you. Well, you have met your match in me. If you don't cough up $22.50 right now, Super Paperboy will rip the roof off your house, reach in, and help himself from your pockets. And you will never receive another Clarion again.

Signed,
Super Paperboy

Well, that's what Alex wanted to write, anyway. But Mom made him be polite.

Dear Clarion Customer,

I'm Alex, your Clarion carrier. Thursday is collection day, but you never seem to be home when I come by to collect. You are now five weeks behind. Please call to arrange a convenient time for me to collect the $22.50 owing for your newspapers. Or you can call the Clarion office to make other arrangements.

Alex signed the notice and wrote his telephone number below his signature. The next day he put it into the mailbox at 141 Abel Avenue. That evening he had a telephone call, and then he went out with Dad.

Customer Never-Home didn't get home from work until six o'clock. He said he would try to put some money in an envelope in the mailbox on Thursdays, and if it wasn't there, Alex was to come back after dinner and he would pay him then. He gave Alex two bills, a twenty and a ten, and told him to keep the change — for his trouble.

Alex dropped the bills on top of the pile of lovely cash in the QBrix container and rubbed his hands together with glee.

He was getting rich!

4
SUPER PAPERBOY GETS HIS SUPER ON

Alex usually kept some change in his pockets. He liked the sound of it clinking around as he walked. But his mom did *not* like the sound of it rattling around in the washer or dryer.

"Either learn to check your pockets before putting your pants in the laundry or I'll start keeping whatever I find," Mom told him. "Tips for the laundress."

After that, Alex was more careful, and left

his money in the QBrix container unless he had a use for it. The day his class had a field trip to the Science Centre he filled both pockets. Mom and Dad believed field trips were for education, not shopping, and they said a packed lunch was healthier than cafeteria food. But today he had convinced them to let him do what so many other kids in his class did: buy lunch and something from the gift shop. It would be the best field trip ever!

The bus ride to the city took over an hour. During that time, Alex counted the contents of his bulging pockets three times, just for something to do.

"Whadja do, rob a bank?" asked his buddy Moh.

"This is my paper route money," said Alex.

"Wow. I gotta get a paper route," said Moh. "Is it hard?"

"Sometimes," said Alex. "You know how I haven't been hanging around after school to shoot hoops lately? That's cuz I have to get home to deliver papers. And I have to get up early on Saturday, too. And I have to do it even when it rains. And I still have to do my homework and chores. So, less time for gaming and stuff."

"Oh," said Moh. "Maybe I'll get one when I'm older."

"You can have a paper route when you bring home three excellent report cards in a row," said Moh's mom, Mrs. Khan, who was sitting right behind them. She always volunteered to be a parent monitor on field trips. "Then we will know you can handle the extra work."

"That'll be never, then," whispered Moh to Alex, and they laughed.

After touring around the Science Centre for a while, Alex's group had an hour before the nature movie was due to begin. When Mrs. Khan let them choose which to do first — lunch or the gift shop — they all voted for the gift shop.

The Science Centre gift shop was one of Alex's favourite places. There were so many cool gadgets to build or play with — wind-up wall crawlers with sticky feet, magnetic spinning globes, clocks that ran on potato power. He picked up one thing after another. At first, it was because he couldn't decide which was best. But after a while, it was because nothing seemed good enough.

"What are you going to get?" asked Moh. His mother had given him five dollars and he had already spent it. Now he was working on getting six ball bearings inside a clear acrylic ball to land in just the right spaces. "You're lucky. I could only get this puzzle . . ." He paused, grimacing, ". . . and I just solved it." He gave the ball a shake.

"I can't decide," said Alex. In the end, he left the shop empty-handed. Nothing there had given him the same feeling of exciting potential as his pockets full of money did.

In the cafeteria, Alex was surprised by how much everything cost. When he was with his parents, everything just looked good. He never really paid attention to the numbers. He finally settled on the cheapest cooked item on the menu: a plate of fries with gravy.

"That is not a good lunch for a growing boy," Mrs. Khan said, and insisted Alex share the box of homemade samosas and chutney she and Moh were eating. They were delicious and very spicy. Alex remembered the ice-cream cooler by the cafeteria cash register.

"I'm getting a Peanut Buddy bar," he said to Moh. "Do you want one? My treat."

Moh looked over at Mrs. Khan. "Can I, Ma?"

"Would you like one, too, Mrs. Khan?" Alex asked politely.

"I would! Me, too!" called the other guys in the group, laughing and jostling Alex and Moh.

Mrs. Khan smiled. "No, thank you, Alex. But Moh may have one, certainly."

There was a sign above the cooler that said:

SPECIAL!

Frootjoosee, 2 for $2.

Alex did the math in his head.

"Hey, Moh, if you're okay with it, we could get all the guys a Frootjoosee for not much more than two Peanut Buddy bars," he said.

"Let's do it!" said Moh.

The purchases emptied one pocket, but Alex didn't care. Handing out those Frootjoosees gave him a great feeling. A *super* feeling.

The next day Alex helped Mrs. Jurgens carry her groceries from the car to the front door. She made a big fuss thanking him, and by the time Alex returned to his route the super feeling had worn off.

Then, on Thursday the next week, Alex was walking along Philip Street when he had to stop. Friday morning was waste collection day in his neighbourhood. On the front porch of the first house a man was feeling for the edge of the porch with his toe. He couldn't see over the blue bins he was carrying, which were full, stacked, and wobbling dangerously. It looked like an accident waiting to happen.

"Can I give you a hand?" called Alex, alarmed.

FOR WEEKS, THERE HAD BEEN NO RAIN, AND THE PEOPLE WERE GASPING WITH THIRST.

THE HOT SUN BEAT DOWN AS THEY TURNED THEIR DUSTY FACES TO THE SKY.

HELP US, SUPER PAPERBOY!

AS SUPER PAPERBOY TOSSED THE STICKS TO THE EAGER VILLAGERS BELOW HIM, CLOUDS GATHERED IN THE SKY ABOVE. THE FIRST DROPS OF RAIN BEGAN TO FALL AND THE VILLAGERS DANCED WITH JOY.

"Sure!" said the man.

Alex helped the man lower the bins to the porch floor. He was the smallest old man Alex had ever seen, with long grey hair and wiry arms covered with tattoos.

"You take this one, sonny. It's light," said the man, and they carried the bins to the curb.

This guy must really like orange pop and canned beef stew, Alex thought.

"Thanks, sonny," said the man, squinting in the late-afternoon sun. Or maybe the squint was permanent. It seemed to go with his tanned, wrinkled face. "Think you got another good deed in you? My bad leg's acting up something fierce today."

Alex had noticed the man limping. "Sure," he said.

He waited nearby while the man dragged the garbage and green bins out of his garage. Together, they carried them out to the street.

"What's your name, sonny?" asked the man.

"Alex."

"Put 'er there. My name's Kevin." The man

pumped Alex's arm up and down. "Thanks a lot, Alex."

"No problem," said Alex. He felt super but also a little embarrassed. It didn't seem like such a big deal, after all. "I gotta finish my paper route now."

"Workin' man, eh? Sure thing," said Kevin, giving Alex's hand one last shake.

On his way back from Carl Avenue, Alex saw Kevin again. He was sitting on his porch steps, rubbing his leg, and grimacing. He looked up and caught Alex's eye.

"Good man, Alex!" Kevin called, and gave him a thumbs-up. "Keep on truckin'!"

Alex waved and headed for home.

The next Thursday, Alex checked out Kevin's place on his way past. Kevin was nowhere to be seen, but there were two full blue bins on the porch. It only took a second for Alex to carry them to the curb. No one saw him do it, so Alex got to enjoy the super feeling all by himself. He didn't even share it with his parents at suppertime.

The moon was full that night. Curled up under the covers, Alex stared sleepily at the QBrix container on his dresser, which was lit up by a ray of moonlight that had slipped between the window curtains. Suddenly, he realized something. The super feeling was familiar. It was joyful and rich. It was just like the feeling he got when he counted his tip money.

Alex smiled. Now Super Paperboy had *two* Secret Sources of Power.

5
SUPER PAPERBOY
OWNS THE WORLD

"Alex!"

Super Paperboy frowned in annoyance. He hated having his planning sessions interrupted.

Mom rapped on the front window. "Alex! Get going! It will be dark soon!"

Alex tucked the Digimart flier back into his parents' paper and put the paper in the mailbox. Then he loaded up his paper bag until it was stuffed full.

It was Wednesday and that meant lots of fliers. Instead of the two or three skinny ones he

AFTER CAREFUL STUDY OF THE ANCIENT SCROLLS AND MYSTICAL MAPS, SUPER PAPERBOY WAS READY. HIS POWERS WERE GROWING DAILY. SOON, HE WOULD LAUNCH HIS ATTACK.

HE WOULD STRIDE INTO THE CASTLE OF WONDERS AND ITS MINIONS WOULD COME RUNNING TO ATTEND HIM, THEIR SPINDLY ARMS WOULD FILL AS HE WENT FROM ROOM TO ROOM, POINTING AT THIS AND THAT.

ONCE HE SETTLED INTO THE ROOM OF THE COUCH, THE CHIEF STEWARD HIMSELF WOULD SEND OUT FOR MEAT AND DRINK, SO THAT SUPER PAPERBOY COULD REFRESH HIMSELF.

THEN THE MINIONS WOULD SCURRY TO UNPACK THE TREASURE CHESTS AND ATTACH THE CABLES OF POWER. AT LAST, ALL WOULD BE READY...

THE CONTROL OF THE WORLD WOULD BE IN SUPER PAPERBOY'S HANDS!

usually got, there were at least five per paper, some with several pages. Sorting and tucking the fliers inside the papers took extra time, and then the papers were so fat Alex could only carry half of them, returning halfway to his front porch to reload.

So, doing his route took Alex almost twice as long on Wednesdays, but he didn't mind. For one thing, every flier put two cents more into his bank account. It didn't sound like much but, multiplied by several fliers and twenty-one customers, it sure added up.

"In fact, any day you have more than six, you're making more money delivering fliers than delivering the actual newspaper," Dad said one evening. He had his accountant game on and had dragged Alex into it, figuring out things like how much he was paid to deliver each paper (twelve cents) and the amount the *Clarion* deducted for his three collection customers (sixty-three cents per paper). "Which means, if you didn't have any fliers at all, your weekly bank deposit would be . . . ?"

"What is this, school?" Alex protested.

"No, it's life, son," Dad said. "'Look after the pennies and the pounds will take care of themselves,' as they say. Or, to paraphrase, 'Look after the dimes and the dollars . . .'" Dad laughed at Alex's weary expression and tousled his hair. "Okay, okay — scoot, then. It's bedtime, anyway."

Alex had stopped minding Wednesday's extra work and time after that. Instead, it became the day when Super Paperboy did his best thinking.

For example, Super Paperboy had invented three useful gadgets on three different Wednesdays, designed to solve three different problems.

The first gadget was a rolling vertical saw for trimming hedges — no lifting required. Alex hated pushing between the hedge and the car in the driveway at 139 Abel Avenue, especially when it rained. The branches got down his neck, and the car was always dirty.

The second gadget was a pair of super-gripping, spring-loaded boots. One of Alex's customers was far away from any of his other customers. Every day, Alex had to walk past four houses to deliver that one paper, then cross the street and walk that same distance again until he got to his next customer. With the boots, he could just press a button, and *pop*! The springs would push him into the air and over the four driveways. He would have just enough time to drop the paper in the mailbox before the springs pulled him back.

The third gadget was based on Alex's Nerf gun. You loaded it with a rolled-up newspaper and shot it into the letter slot, right past the savage Yapper Snapper and into the Caves of Clafooey. Lately, Super Paperboy had been working on some refinements to this gadget. How, for example, could he arrange it so that the gun delivered the paper to the customer and gave a nasty electric shock to the Yapper Snapper at the same time?

Such thoughts kept Super Paperboy entertained on his Wednesday round, and solved problems that troubled paperboys everywhere.

But sometimes only one problem occupied Super Paperboy's mind. It was a problem that concerned only him (and Alex). It was a problem with many possible solutions, none of which was perfect enough.

And the problem was this: How was Super Paperboy (a.k.a. Alex) going to spend his money?

Alex loved his money. Nothing gave him the same good feeling as looking at that pile of cash. Someday, he'd want to spend it. But ever since that day at the Science Centre, he knew that when he did, whatever he bought with it had to be at least as precious as the money was.

By now, Alex had saved enough to start taking the Digimart flier seriously. Every Wednesday he looked at what was being offered. Sometimes it was lower prices. Sometimes it was throw-ins — buy a Velociport 3DX and get a free game, for example. Sometimes it was manufacturer's rebates, which meant you had to mail in a copy of your receipt, and then the company that made the thing you bought would send you some money back.

Whatever the deal, Alex saw that there were ways to get more for less. You just had to decide what you wanted, then wait for the right deal to come along.

And that was the problem. The longer you waited, the more you saved. And the more you saved, the more you could buy, and the more things you wanted.

Alex considered the contents of today's Digimart flier. Maybe he should abandon the Velociport upgrades and go for a Playdock instead. He was halfway there already, and if the tips at Christmas were as good as Dad said, he'd have enough before the end of the year. He still had his birthday money, and with Christmas money from Grandpa and Grandma and Oma and Opa, he could really take advantage of the Boxing Day deals . . .

Alex plunged his hand into his newspaper bag and looked up to see where he was. And got a nasty surprise.

SUPER PAPERBOY REACHED DOWN AND SLAPPED SHUT THE ELECTROMAGNETIC CLIPS AT HIS ANKLES.

SUPER-GRIPPING, SPRING-LOADED BOOTS PHASE 2 ARE READY FOR BETA TESTING.

ALL SYSTEMS ARE GO!

SUPER PAPERBOY MADE SURE HIS PAPER BAG WAS FIRMLY ON HIS SHOULDER. LEFT LEG UNDER HIM FOR BALANCE, HE LEANED BACKWARD SLIGHTLY AND FLEXED HIS THIGH MUSCLES. TODAY WAS THE DAY HE WOULD CLEAR FOUR DRIVEWAYS IN A SINGLE BOUND.

READY...

SET...

SUPER PAPERBOY TOOK A DEEP BREATH. HE LOOKED UP—

AND FROZE!

GASP!

6
SUPER PAPERBOY MEETS HIS DOOM

There was a posse of teenagers in the driveway of 149 Abel Avenue, and they were all staring at Alex.

Alex knew a few good teenagers. At the Y, for example, there was Ryan, who helped out with the open-gym basketball practices on Sunday afternoon. He was great, and he was a teenager. And Alex's usual babysitter was a teenager. But she was a girl.

Teenagers like this — boys, in groups . . .

A FOUR-HEADED GARGANTUAN WAS BLOCKING HIS WAY. IT HAD MONSTROUS HANDS AND FEET. EACH HEAD HAD A BLACK CAP, SPROUTING LANK HAIR. EACH MOUTH WAS OPEN IN A MENACING LAUGH.

AND EACH SET OF EYES WAS STARING STRAIGHT AT HIM!

well, Alex had had some bad experiences with them: in the schoolyard, at the ice rink, and in the Y pool. Mocking and teasing. Shoving and splashing. And that was when Alex was with his friends. Who knew what these guys might do to a small guy like Alex, all alone? Alex didn't know, and not knowing made him nervous.

Alex still felt like he was wearing special boots. But now they were super-gripping, *lead-lined* boots, so heavy that he could barely lift them off the ground. Yet, he had to go on. The *Clarion* must be delivered, whatever the threat.

Alex shuffled forward.

Nothing happened — but the teenagers still stared.

Alex crossed the first driveway diagonally, so that by the time he reached the driveway of number 151, he was at the curb, as far from the posse of teenagers as possible.

One of the teenagers said something to another, and the whole posse laughed. Were they planning to jump him? Would they steal his papers? Would they rough him up, just for something to do?

Grimly, Alex kept walking. The teenagers all turned their heads, watching him every step of the way, over the third driveway and up the fourth. They watched him walk up the pathway to his customer's front door. Alex felt their eyes drilling holes in his back as he folded the paper and put it into the mailbox.

Alex kept his eyes on his feet all the way back to the curb. Then he lifted his head. He looked across the street. He looked left. Finally, he looked right.

And caught the eye of the tallest teenager, the one who had made a comment before. He growled, "See you tomorrow, *paperboy*."

The posse laughed.

"Run," whispered Alex's feet.

With every gram of will he had, Alex walked across the street, one super-gripping, lead-lined step after another. He delivered two more papers on Abel Avenue, then turned the corner onto Philip Street. One paper here, one paper there, and the posse was out of sight.

And then Alex ran. Alex had never done his Carl Avenue deliveries so quickly. When he got home, he was panting.

His dad came in the door as Alex was taking off his hat and coat.

"Are you okay, son?" he asked.

"Yes. I was just running," Alex said.

"Fitness and finance," said Dad. "Aren't paper routes great?"

"Yeah," said Alex. "Great."

Alex did his homework. He practiced piano. He ate supper, cleared the table, and helped Dad with the dishes.

"I got a lead on some great comic books online. Want to help me pick some?" Dad asked when they were done. Shopping for comics usually put Dad in the mood to look at his favourite Superman oldies, which meant Alex got to pick one and withdraw it, very carefully, from its plastic sleeve so that they could read it together. But neither Dad nor Superman could help Super Paperboy now.

"No, thanks," said Alex. "I think I'll go to bed."

He took a shower. He brushed his teeth and put on his pyjamas.

Mom came in to say goodnight.

"You've been quiet all night. Do you have something on your mind?"

"Yes," said Alex.

"Anything I can help you with?"

"I'll let you know."

"Okay. Well, goodnight, then."

Alex lay in the dark and stared at the ceiling. He had it all figured out. He knew what the posse was planning to do.

That guy had said, "See you tomorrow." How had he known that tomorrow was collection day? Had the posse been watching Alex, all these weeks — scoping him out and biding their time?

Tomorrow they would act. Alex was sure of it. It was no coincidence that they had gathered there, on the driveway of 149 Abel Avenue. They knew that when Alex crossed that driveway tomorrow, his pockets would be full of money, collected from 137, 141, and 145.

Alex knew how it worked. He watched TV. He read books. He leafed through magazines at the dentist's office. He knew how you had to pay a gang not to beat you up. "Protection" it was called. Very funny choice of word, when the thing they were protecting you from was themselves. Well, tomorrow was collection day, that was for sure. For Alex's customers, and for Alex: because tomorrow, that posse of teenagers was going to start collecting protection money.

And Alex could kiss all his profits goodbye.

Alex turned on his lamp and got out of bed to fetch his QBrix container. He emptied all his cash onto his duvet and counted it, slowly and lovingly. Then he put the QBrix container back on his desk and got back into bed. He turned off his lamp.

As of tomorrow, the pile of cash would start shrinking. Alex's collections would be skimmed by the posse and the money in the container would get spent on this, that, and the other thing. Eventually, Alex would have only his pitiful allowance and the invisible, untouchable bank account.

"Goodnight, lovely cash. And goodbye," Alex whispered.

7
DOOMSDAY

Alex was tempted to stay and play ball with the guys after school the next day. But it would just delay the unavoidable. So, he went home at his usual time. He unpacked his knapsack, as usual, and ate the snack his mom put out for him.

On his way to the front door he poked his head into her office.

"I'm going out on my paper route now," he said.

Mom looked up from her work.

"All right. Collection day today. Need any change?" she said.

"No." Alex paused.

"Yes?" his mom asked.

Alex rushed in and put his arms around his mother. This was not usual.

Mom hugged him back. "What's this for?" she asked.

"It's, uh, National Hug Your Mom Day," he said. "See you later."

Today's paper was a light one. It didn't take long to load up. Alex trudged down his front walk and turned left. He saw his mom through the office window, head bent, scribbling away. He waved, but she didn't look up.

Alex had never felt so alone.

Mrs. Jurgens at 137 Abel Avenue had just baked cookies.

"Would you like one, Alex?" she asked.

"No, thanks," said Alex. The snack he'd had at home felt like a ball of Plasticine in his stomach.

"That's right, sonny, you should check with your mother first," said Mrs. Jurgens. "Wait right here."

Mrs. Jurgens disappeared down the hallway. She came back with six cookies in a Zipshut bag, which she slipped into his coat pocket.

"You can have those for dessert tonight," she said. Then she counted out the week's newspaper money into Alex's hand, like she always did.

Alex thanked her and went on his way. He hoped Frank at 141 had forgotten his envelope, so that Alex could come back after supper with his dad. But, no — the envelope was there, with a five-dollar bill inside. Darn.

Ms. Jain at 145 was digging through her purse when she came to the door.

"I seem to be short this week, Alex," she said, handing him a toonie. "Can I add the rest to next week's collection?"

Yes! Alex thought. "Do you know what, Ms. Jain?" he said. "I'll cover for you this week. You know, out of all the tips you've given me." He handed the toonie back. The less money he was carrying, the less the posse would get. And the less they got this week, the less interested they would be next week. He hoped.

"Really? Are you sure?" Ms. Jain looked very surprised.

"Yup."

"Okay, Alex. Thanks!"

She seemed so happy, Alex felt a little bad. He wished he'd made the offer for a better reason. "See you next week, Ms. Jain," he said.

Ms. Jain lightly touched his head. "You're a real sweetie, you know that?"

She closed the door.

Only one more delivery to go, before Alex had to face the posse at 149. As he was walking back down the steps of 147 Abel Avenue, he peeked sideways. The posse was there, all right. And even though they weren't looking at him, Alex was sure they had seen him.

Alex reached into his coat pocket, feeling for his money. Instead, he felt the cool smoothness of plastic. It was the bag of cookies. He was about to feel in his other pocket when something stopped him. This was a posse of teenagers. And teenagers were always hungry — weren't they?

"*The best defence is a good offence*," whispered Super Paperboy.

Alex took a deep breath. He marched over the first driveway, heading right for the posse.

"Hey!" he said.

The tallest teenager turned his head with a jerk.

"Do you want some cookies?"

All the teenagers turned to look. Alex waved the bag.

"One of my customers gave me some cookies. Do you want them?"

The tallest teenager looked at the others, and shrugged.

Alex thrust the bag into his hand.

"Here, take them."

Without a backward glance, Alex marched on, over the third and fourth driveways and right up the steps to the mailbox of 155. He pushed the paper inside. He turned around, and marched straight to the curb. He checked for traffic: left, right, left. All clear. Straight as a soldier, he marched across the street, left, right, left, right, and delivered his papers on the other side.

SUPER PAPERBOY TOSSED THE FOUR-HEADED GARGANTUAN SOME RAW MEAT AND THE STARVING CREATURE JUMPED UPON IT!

SUPER PAPERBOY LEAPED OVER THE GATE.

HE WAS IN! THE CASTLE OF WONDERS WAS OPEN!

Only when Alex was at the corner of Philip and Abel did he glance back.

The posse was laughing and horsing around. And on the ground, an empty Zipshut bag fluttered in the wind.

8
THE NAME OF POWER

Alex felt great — more than great. He felt super! He bounded through the rest of his deliveries and came home with more energy than when he'd left. There was spaghetti and meatballs for supper, and he ate three helpings — more than Dad. He did his homework in record time. When it was time to help Dad sort the recycling, he volunteered to do it all himself. Dad only had to help him carry it out to the curb.

"To what do I owe this honour?" Dad asked.

"It's National Help Your Dad Day," Alex said.

Alex still felt great the next morning. He felt great all day, even when he saw the huge stack waiting for him on his front porch. Christmas was coming, and the *Clarion* was piling on the fliers. Oh, well. The more fliers there were, the more money Alex made. Which was good, because Christmas was coming after all.

Alex's great feeling dimmed a little as he set off. But as soon as he got to the top of the Abel Avenue hill, the great feeling returned. The driveway at 149 was empty.

When Alex got back, supper was on the table, and Mom and Dad were waiting. Alex washed his hands quickly and sat down.

"Any homework tonight?" Dad asked.

"Nope," Alex said.

"How about a movie, then?"

"Great!" said Alex.

Dad did the dishes alone so that Alex could walk with Mom up to Mayneway Convenience to get some movie snacks. Mom and Dad prided themselves on using the car as little as possible. Dad rode his bike or walked to work, and Mom mostly worked at home. When she had meetings in the city, she took the bus.

Alex wished they could drive. So that they could zip right by 149 Abel Avenue. Even thinking about the place gave him a stomach ache.

"Don't you want to go to the grocery store? You always say snack food is cheaper there," he said, as they got ready.

"How many snacks do you think we're going to buy? Anyway, I could use the walk. Ready? Let's go!"

Alex sighed. Mom might have been sitting at her desk all day, but Alex's feet were still tired from doing his paper route. And his boots were wet.

As they walked, they noticed some people had already put up their Christmas lights.

"It's only the middle of November!" said Mom. "The Christmas fuss gets earlier every year. Have you got any Christmas tips yet?"

"Nope," said Alex.

"Oh, look — those are pretty," Mom commented. She was pointing at 145 Abel Avenue.

Alex had noticed the three deer on the lawn earlier. They were made of twigs or something, and now Alex could see they were covered with little white lights.

Ms. Jain's front door opened, and a boy came out, calling, "Bye!"

Then Ms. Jain came to the door, with something in her hand. In the light from the front hall, Alex saw her lift a toque high — the boy was taller than she was — and put it on the boy's head. Then she stood on her toes and kissed him on the forehead.

The boy jerked back, and Ms. Jain laughed and grabbed his jacket. "Bye-bye, Sweetie-Pie!" she said.

"Mo-om!" the boy said, and Ms. Jain let go. But the boy called over his shoulder as he went down the steps, "So long, Mini-Mom!"

"Isn't that cute, Alex? Alex?"

Mom was on the far side of Ms. Jain's

driveway. She turned to stare at her son. Alex was frozen to the sidewalk. And standing between them, on Ms. Jain's driveway, was the tallest teenager from the posse.

Ms. Jain's son.

Sweetie-Pie.

Sweetie-Pie's face turned very red. His eyes locked on Alex's, and he took a step forward.

Alex stepped back, his eyes locked on Sweetie-Pie's. Sweetie-Pie raised one arm.

Just then a car pulled up, and Sweetie-Pie glanced over. His arm dropped, and, with a last look at Alex, he darted to the car. He got in and the car drove away.

"Alex? Who was that?" Mom asked. "Is he one of your newspaper customers?"

"Uh, yeah. No. Sort of," Alex said, in a daze.

Sweetie-Pie.

All weekend long, Alex's mind went round and round that name. The leader of the posse Alex dreaded and feared was somebody's son. Like him, Alex. That tall, loud teenager was somebody's "Sweetie-Pie," the way Alex was his mother's "Smart Alecky" and his father's "Chipster."

Alex wondered what Sweetie-Pie's real name was. Steven? Paul? Did the members of his posse know what his mother called him? Alex didn't think so. But maybe they were all keeping secrets like that. Every teenager had at least one parent. Did that mean that every teenager had at least one silly nickname that only their families knew?

At the Y that Sunday, Alex volunteered to help put the basketballs away after practice.

"Ryan," he said, "can I ask you something?"

"Shoot, Alex," said Ryan.

"Do you have a nickname? Like, do your parents call you anything . . . embarrassing?"

Ryan got a funny look on his face.

"I won't tell anyone," Alex promised. "It's just . . . I really need to know."

Ryan looked around, then leaned in close.

"My mom calls me Cupcake," he whispered. "I'm her little cupcake with the frosting on the top. On account of my hair, you know." Ryan's

SUPER PAPERBOY KNEW THE FOUR-HEADED GARGANTUAN'S NAME OF POWER NOW. HE HAD ONLY TO WHISPER IT, AND THE FOUR SETS OF SNARLING, TOOTH-PACKED JAWS WOULD DROOL HELPLESSLY.

THE FOUR HUGE HEADS WOULD LIE DOWN IN THE DUST, AND SUPER PAPERBOY WOULD STEP OVER THEM WITHOUT FEAR OF HARM. AND THE CASTLE OF WONDERS WOULD BE HIS TO ENJOY — FOREVER.

hair was amazing. It surrounded his head like a dark, dense thundercloud. Or like thick frosting on a double-chocolate cupcake.

"Wow," breathed Alex.

Ryan frowned. "But if this gets out, I know where to find you. So keep it to yourself, dude!"

"I will," Alex promised again. They shook on it.

9
EPIC FAIL

On Monday, Moh came home with Alex after school. His parents were in the city and wouldn't be home until late, so Moh was sleeping over. It was the first time Alex had a friend along when he did his route. It was great. There were so many fliers now, every day was like Wednesday. With Moh helping, though, sorting and tucking went way faster.

While they worked, Alex told Moh all about his changing purchase plans.

"Woah, First World problems, dude," said Moh. He had some good advice, though, and by the time they were ready to set off (with Moh carrying some of the newspapers in two grocery bags) Alex had made a decision. He was going to get a Playdock system. With all his QBrix savings and the Christmas money his grandparents always sent, he'd have enough. And if he could persuade his parents to take him to Digimart on Boxing Day in time for the early-bird specials, he might get a throw-in game, as well.

"And then, as soon as we get back from my aunt's place, you gotta come over and play," said Alex. "Brendan and the guys, too. Bring your games and we can play all day. It'll be awesome!"

They were so busy making plans that Alex didn't think about the posse until they reached number 149. Then he remembered about Sweetie-Pie. He took a deep breath and led Moh straight toward the posse, glancing to the right as they passed.

Sweetie-Pie was looking right at him.

"Thanks for the cookies, kid," he said. "Mrs. Jurgens, right?"

Alex stood still.

"Number 137? Always right on the dot with the payments?"

Alex's feet and hands went cold. The posse *had* been watching him.

"Convenient — but not too profitable, eh? Not like some places." The teenager laughed, and the rest of the posse joined in obediently. "Tips — the paperboy's secret," he said. He turned back to Alex. "Don't worry, kid. *I'll* keep *your* secret."

He stared hard at Alex, eyes narrowed. "See you Thursday, paperboy," he said.

"Woah. Who *are* those dudes?" whispered Moh. "They're, like, really scary. And that one guy? The one who talked to you? What's his deal? It's like he was mad at you or something."

"Long story," said Alex. "Can we talk about something else?"

That night, after Moh had dropped off to sleep, Alex lay awake, thinking. Sweetie-Pie had made himself pretty clear: as long as Alex kept his secret, Alex's collection money was safe.

For now, anyway. Because really, what

BUT BEFORE SUPER PAPERBOY COULD SPEAK THE NAME OF POWER, THE FOUR-HEADED GARGANTUAN CAME AT HIM, THE FOUR SETS OF JAWS SNAPPING, THE FOUR THROATS SNARLING.

SUPER PAPERBOY DUCKED, THEN ROLLED AWAY, AS THE GATES OF THE CASTLE OF WONDERS CLANGED SHUT!

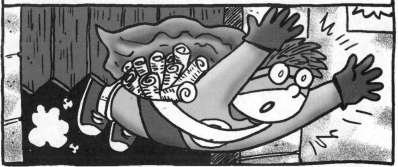

HE'D GO AFTER ITS TREASURES ANOTHER DAY. FOR NOW, SUPER PAPERBOY WAS JUST GRATEFUL TO ESCAPE WITH HIS LIFE.

could Alex do if the posse decided otherwise? Alex could just imagine it: Super Paperboy trying to squeak out the Name of Power while Gargantuan's four sets of teeth were ripping his throat out. Alex himself, squeaking out, "Hey, Sweetie-Pie! Your mother wants you!" just before the posse jumped him. Would they stop, mid-pummel? Would they back away in horror? No. They'd jam his paper bag over his head, empty his pockets, and send him on his feeble way.

So, for the rest of the week, Alex scuttled past the posse of teenagers in the driveway of 149 Abel Avenue, head down, eyes on his boots. On Thursday, he felt Sweetie-Pie's eyes on him all the way, and didn't breathe easy until he was on Philip Street.

Kevin was standing on his driveway. As they carried the bins to the curb, he asked, "Everything okay, Alex? You look like you've got a storm cloud over your head."

Alex was afraid of what might come bursting out of that storm cloud if he talked about it.

"I'm okay," he said. "Just one of those days. You know."

The dog behind the door at 132 Carl Avenue was in overdrive, yapping and whining.

"Shut up, you dumb dog. You give me a headache," Alex said, and trudged homeward.

10
SUPER PAPERBOY RETURNS — FOR A MOMENT

Winter arrived that weekend. On Saturday morning, a cold wind blew hard pellets of snow right in Alex's face as he was going up the Abel Avenue hill. Then the wind changed direction, so that it could keep peppering him with snow pellets on the way back down.

Alex thought of all his friends, sleeping in, all cozy and warm, while he had to trudge through the chilly streets, with the wind trying to push him down every time he turned a corner. They thought Alex was lucky, with his pockets always jingling. They had no idea of the sacrifices he had to make.

"Alex, your face is as red as a beet!" his mother exclaimed when he came in.

Alex could barely move his jaw. "Hot tloco-late," he moaned. "Tlease."

Sunday there was no paper, thank goodness. Overnight, the snow pellets turned to flakes. When Alex went to school on Monday morning, the snow was higher than his ankles. By the time he got home it was knee deep and Alex was already exhausted from pushing through it. He thought that if he sat down, he wouldn't be able to get up again. So he handed his mother his knapsack, took his paper bag and the snack she gave him, and loaded up right away.

There was one good thing about the snow, at least, Alex thought as he slogged along. It kept the posse inside.

The snow stopped, and Tuesday morning was bright and sunny. On Tuesday afternoon, the posse was back, pelting one another with snowballs as Alex passed by. A big one landed on Alex's head, knocking his toque right off.

"Score!" one of the teenagers shouted, and they all laughed.

Alex picked up his toque and shook the snow off. But there must have been some snow inside still, melting. Because as Alex walked, something watery ran down his face. Alex scrubbed at the wetness angrily, and his snow-covered mittens left an icy track down his cheek.

The snow returned in the night and kept falling, off and on, through the morning. While Alex was doing his route, the snow turned to sleet. The snow on the ground got mushier and mushier. Alex's paper bag was made of thick, water-repellent canvas, but still, the last fliers Alex delivered that Wednesday were downright wet. When Alex got home, his boots, snowpants, coat, hat, and mittens were all soaked through, and he couldn't stop shivering.

His mom ran a hot bath and made him get in it. She gave him chicken soup for supper, specially, and sent him to bed early. *Too early*, Alex thought, and got out his book — and then fell asleep before he had read a page.

Overnight, the cold wind returned. Everything froze. In the morning, Alex's mom called the school. The school buses weren't running because of the icy roads. A lot of kids would be absent that day. Mom let Alex stay home, too.

Alex felt fine after lunch. He decided to do his paper route early.

"Do you want to wait until Dad comes home, so he can help you?" Mom asked anxiously.

"Naw. I'd rather just get it done," Alex said.

Mom brought him his outdoor clothes, all dried, even his boots. She had washed and dried his paper bag, too.

"I'm not sure I should have — it got awfully ravelled inside," she commented, handing him the bag.

Alex saw what she meant when he loaded up. The bag was filled with long threads, which tangled around his hands every time he got a paper out.

The walk was very difficult. The cold wind was still blowing in sideways gusts, and the sidewalk was incredibly slippery. Alex fell down going up the hill so many times that he ended up crawling in places. He began to wish he *had* waited for Dad.

Mr. Jurgens was outside, salting the front steps, when Alex arrived.

"Nothing can stop the faithful carrier from completing his appointed rounds, eh?" he said to Alex. He looked around, then reached into his pocket. "You deserve something extra, for getting out early on a day like this." He pressed a loonie into Alex's mittened hand. "From me to you. No need to tell Mrs. Jurgens, eh?" He winked, and went back to his salting.

Alex rang the doorbell, and Mrs. Jurgens bustled to the door.

"Here already, and on such a day? What service!" she cried. "I don't even have your money ready yet!"

Alex waited while she counted out the right sum, first from her purse to the hall table, then from the table into his hand.

"You're a good boy, Alex," she said, and then, to his surprise, she added another loonie. "Such bad weather — you deserve it," she said. "I'm sure Mr. Jurgens would agree."

There was an envelope waiting for him in the mailbox at 141. In it was a note:

Alex,

I'll be away for most of December and I'll be really busy until then, so in case I forget, can you remember to stop my paper Dec. 6th? I'll be back on the 27th.

Frank

P.S. The enclosed should cover it from now till then, plus tip. Merry Christmas!

The note was folded around a fifty-dollar bill.

Fifty dollars!

Reverently, Alex folded the note back around the bill, put them into the envelope and tucked the envelope into his paper bag. A grin spread across his face. He was *definitely* getting the Playdock!

Heck, he could get a Playdock *plus* at least two games. Which ones should he get? There were so many great RPGs out there. But nothing too bloody — he didn't like that. And nothing with grown up looking girls. Yuck.

Lost in planning, Alex had rung the bell at 145 about a dozen times before he realized no one was home. That's right — he was early today. And that meant — he looked, just to make sure — yes! The posse wasn't there, either! Alex looked at his watch. The high school was blocks away. If he hurried, he'd be well along Philip Street before they even came around the corner from Mayneway Boulevard.

Slipping and sliding and keeping an eye on the street corner, Alex crossed the four driveways and deposited a paper at 155. Just before he crossed Abel Avenue, he took a last look over

his shoulder. The high school must have let out earlier than he thought, because there was the posse, coming along Mayneway and about to turn the corner!

"Hey, kid! Stop! STOP!"

Too late, Alex saw the car heading straight for him.

11
THE HIGH PRICE OF PROTECTION

Fortunately, the roads were bad and the car was headed uphill, so the driver was going slowly.

Unfortunately, as soon as the driver slammed on his brakes, the car began to fishtail, and Alex didn't know which way to turn. He chose, and ran.

Fortunately, he chose correctly.

Unfortunately, he slipped.

Fortunately, he managed to get up.

Unfortunately, his paper bag split open, and the papers went flying.

Fortunately, Alex managed to catch a few.

Unfortunately, most of them got away. And Alex lost it. He slumped down onto the curb and began to cry.

"Are you okay? I didn't hit you, did I?" The driver's face loomed over him.

Alex shook his head. "M-my p-papers," he sobbed.

The driver crouched down and put his arm around Alex. "It's okay, kid. Your buddies will get them. Just tell me — are you okay?"

Alex stared at the man. "My b-buddies?"

"Look," said the driver. He moved aside.

The posse had scattered. Darting here, darting there — slipping, falling — grabbing. All of them laughing. Gathering Alex's papers, folding them, putting them back in his bag and wrapping the strap around them so they wouldn't fall out.

"I-I'm okay," said Alex. "You didn't hit me. I just fell. I'm okay."

"Thank God," said the driver. "Do you live around here? Can you get home all right? I can give you a lift if you need it."

"No, I'll be okay."

"You sure?" The driver studied Alex for a while, then nodded. "Well, I guess your buddies will look after you. Take care, now."

He got back in his car, and drove slowly away.

Ms. Jain's son dumped the bundled bag and papers onto Alex's lap.

"Now that's what I call collecting," he said. "I think we got them all."

Alex looked up. "Thanks," he said.

"No problem," said another of the teenagers.

"Gotta go now," said the third.

"Good luck with the rest of your route," said the fourth.

They slipped and slid across the road, and Alex watched them disappear into the mysterious depths of 149 Abel Avenue.

And then Alex remembered his envelope.

He hurried home and told his mother what had happened. She told him he was not to finish his deliveries.

"Your father can take care of it when he gets home," she said. "You just relax, honey."

But before Alex could relax, he had to know for sure. Telling his mother he had to check in case some bits had been lost, he searched every paper. He even searched the bag again, but without hope.

Alex's fifty-dollar bill, the note, the envelope — all were gone.

Alex didn't know what to think. The posse had been so *great*. They had seen the danger and had tried to stop him from crossing the road. Then, without him even asking, they had gone after all his scattered papers. They had folded them and put them safely in his bag. And they'd done it with laughter. When they had returned the papers to him, they had seemed, not like scary teenagers, but like . . . like friends.

On the other hand, the envelope was gone. The posse had found all the newspapers, no matter where the wind had blown them. How could they have missed his envelope? It had been one of those yellowy-brown ones. Surely it would have stood out against the snow?

Alex was forced to conclude that the posse *had* found the envelope — and that they had kept it. That was the price of protection — fifty bucks a month. That was the cost of their help, their supposed kindness.

Alex remembered what Sweetie-Pie had said when he gave Alex his papers back: "That's what I call collecting." Probably, at that moment, Sweetie-Pie had been planning what he was going to do with the sweet fifty dollars he had in his pocket. *Alex's* fifty dollars.

Alex couldn't help feeling bitter, especially when he remembered that the fifty was supposed to cover Frank's paper for the next few weeks. So Alex would be paying for that, as well. Huh!

The posse wasn't there the next day, and Alex was almost sorry. He had never punched anyone in his life, with or without Super Paperboy. But today, if Alex had glared at the teenagers in passing and they had jumped him for it, well, at least he could have gotten a few blows in

SUPER PAPERBOY SEIZED ONE HEAD IN A DEATH VISE GRIP. THE OTHER THREE HEADS HOWLED AND NATTERED AND BIT AT HIS HEAD AND SHOULDERS...

HE IGNORED THEM AND, WITH A MIGHTY HEAVE, WRESTLED THE FOUR-HEADED GARGANTUAN TO THE GROUND, EXPOSING ITS SOFT BELLY.

HE JUMPED, AND THE GARGANTUAN GASPED FOR MERCY!

himself before he was beaten to a pulp. What a relief that would be!

Alex was in his room, staring glumly at his Velociport (he'd never get a Velociport 3DX, much less a Playdock, he was positive) when the doorbell rang. After a bit, Mom stuck her head in.

"Alex, there's someone at the door for you," she said. She added, in a whisper, "I think it's that boy we saw the other night."

Alex felt his eyes go wide. Sweetie-Pie, here? What did he want — more money?

Alex had had enough. Posse or no posse, Alex was going to tell that darn Sweetie-Pie just where he could go!

12

GOOD GAME, SUPER PAPERBOY

Alex marched to the front door.

"What do you want?" he said, as rudely as he could.

"I think this is yours," Sweetie-Pie said. In his hand was a yellowy-brown envelope. "I found it in a bush."

Alex stared in amazement.

"The money's still inside, in case you were wondering," said Sweetie-Pie.

Alex took the envelope and looked inside. The fifty was there, all right, safe and sound.

"Your posse — I thought . . ." Alex trailed off because of the look on Sweetie-Pie's face.

"My *what?*"

"Y-your posse," said Alex. "I thought you took the money as payment for helping me with my papers. And for protection."

Sweetie-Pie looked at Alex in amazement. "For *protection?* What the . . . ?"

Then Sweetie-Pie started to laugh. He laughed and laughed. He laughed so hard, he started to hiccup, and Alex had to run to the kitchen to get him a drink of water.

"So, let me — *hic* — get this straight," said Sweetie-Pie at last. "You thought we were some kind of . . . gang? And that we were planning to jump you?"

Alex nodded.

"What in heck made you think that?"

Alex didn't know what to say. "You're teenagers" didn't seem like enough of an answer; neither did "You're all so big, and you laugh so loud." But Alex had to give him some kind of explanation.

"You kept calling me 'paperboy' and laughing," Alex said, looking at the floor.

"Okay, we kind of dissed you. But we were just goofing around."

"You knew so much about my route. About Mrs. Jurgens, and collecting . . . I thought you'd been watching me."

Pause.

Alex looked up.

Sweetie-Pie was grinning. "I used to *have* your route, kid. And I always loved Mrs. Jurgens's cookies. My mom never bakes."

Alex suddenly felt like he had to sit down.

"Do you want to come in?" he asked Sweetie-Pie. "I think my dad's taking something out of the oven, right now."

Sweetie-Pie took off his boots and jacket. He called his mom to let her know he'd be awhile. Then he sat down at Alex's dining room table and wolfed down six cookies and two glasses of milk while Alex told him everything.

Everything minus Super Paperboy, that is.

"And then, the day after I saw you that

night, with your mom . . ." Alex said.

"Uh, yeah. About that . . ." Sweetie-Pie stopped laughing. "I really was trying to scare you then, kid. I definitely don't want the whole Sweetie-Pie thing to get around, okay? I just wanted to make sure you kept it to yourself."

"Oh, I will," Alex assured him. Then he asked, "What *is* your name, anyway?"

Sweetie-Pie laughed again. "Mackenzie. Mac, to my friends. What's yours?"

"Alex."

Sweetie-Pie stuck out his fist. "Nice to meet you, Alex."

Alex bumped the fist with his own. "You, too, Mackenzie."

Sweetie-Pie shook his head. "Please. I told you — my friends call me Mac."

Alex grinned. "Okay, Mac," he said.

While Sweetie-Pie — no, Mac — polished off another half-dozen cookies, they shared paper route stories.

"Is that dog still howling away at 132 Carl Avenue?" Mac asked.

"I wouldn't call it a howl," said Alex.

"Black-and-brown thing, really big?" Mac asked.

"No — small and white. A real yapper snapper," said Alex.

"Must have got a new one, then," said Mac, and he shook his head. "Man, this sure brings it all back." He pushed his chair back and got up. "Thanks for the cookies, Mr. Vriend," he called.

Alex was startled. "Do you know my dad?" he asked.

"Alex — I used to *own* this street, remember? Just like you do now." He punched Alex on the shoulder, in a painful but friendly kind of way.

Going out the door, Mac turned. "Say, kid, if you ever need a sub, let me know," he said. "I remember how tough it was, finding someone to take over when me and my mom went on holidays."

This was something Alex had not thought of. And Christmas was coming.

"Thanks, Mac. That would be great," he said.

"It'll cost ya, though," Mac growled.

"Sure, sure," said Alex. Then, lowering his voice, he added, "Whatever it takes, Sweetie-Pie."

Super Paperboy closed the door, quickly, on Mac's startled face.

THE VILLAGE IS AT PEACE, ITS INHABITANTS RECOVERING FROM ITS DAYS OF CELEBRATING AND FEASTING.

HIGH ON THE HILL, THE CASTLE OF WONDERS IS QUIET, THE MINIONS MOVING SLOWLY THROUGH ITS DIM, HALF-EMPTY ROOMS.

THE LAIR OF SUPER PAPERBOY IS CROWDED WITH TREASURE, BUT LIES QUIET AND DARK.

LAIR

FOR SUPER PAPERBOY IS FAR AWAY, RESTING WITH COMMON FOLK WHO HAVE NO IDEA OF HIS SECRET IDENTITY. HIS POWERS ARE SPENT FOR THE MOMENT, BUT SOON HE WILL REBUILD — IN THIS, AND OTHER WORLDS.

IN THE VILLAGE, A WHIRLWIND.

AS IT NEARS, A FIGURE CAN BE SEEN, ITS LEGS A BLUR.

DELIVERIES ARE BEING MADE, AND THEY ARE BEING MADE AT LIGHTNING SPEED. THE CAPED CARRIER RIDES AGAIN— FASTER THAN EVER, STRONGER THAN EVER.

THE TIME HE HAS SPENT IN RETIREMENT HAS ONLY SERVED TO SHARPEN HIS SKILLS. OLDER, WILIER, HE CRISS-CROSSES THE STREET WITH A LAUGH, DARING THE TRAFFIC TO APPROACH HIM.

DARK COMES ON, BUT THE CAPED CARRIER FEARS NOTHING.
EVEN THE SAVAGE YAPPER SNAPPER CAN'T MAKE HIM TREMBLE.

AND NOW, THE CAPED CARRIER IS NEARING HIS HUMBLE ABODE. OTHER REWARDS WILL COME HIS WAY, OF THIS HE IS CERTAIN. FOR NOW, HE REVELS IN THE GLORY OF A JOB WELL DONE. HE LIFTS THE BADGE OF OFFICE FROM HIS SHOULDER, OPENS THE DOOR, AND—

AUGGHH! ALL THE CAPED CARRIER'S POWERS FALL AWAY!